A Note to Parents and Caregivers:

*Read-it!* Readers are for children who are just starting on the amazing road to reading. These beautiful books support both the acquisition of reading skills and the love of books.

 The PURPLE LEVEL presents basic topics and objects using high frequency words and simple language patterns.

 The RED LEVEL presents familiar topics using common words and repeating sentence patterns.

 The BLUE LEVEL presents new ideas using a larger vocabulary and varied sentence structure.

 The YELLOW LEVEL presents more challenging ideas, a broad vocabulary, and wide variety in sentence structure.

 The GREEN LEVEL presents more complex ideas, an extended vocabulary range, and expanded language structures.

 The ORANGE LEVEL presents a wide range of ideas and concepts using challenging vocabulary and complex language structures.

When sharing a book with your child, read in short stretches, pausing often to talk about the pictures. Have your child turn the pages and point to the pictures and familiar words. And be sure to reread favorite stories or parts of stories.

There is no right or wrong way to share books with children. Find time to read with your child, and pass on the legacy of literacy.

Adria F. Klein, Ph.D.
Professor Emeritus
California State University
San Bernardino, California

Editor: Patricia Stockland
Page production: Melissa Kes/JoAnne Nelson/Tracy Davies
Art Director: Keith Griffin
Managing Editor: Catherine Neitge
The illustrations in this book were rendered in acrylic.

Picture Window Books
5115 Excelsior Boulevard
Suite 232
Minneapolis, MN 55416
877-845-8392
www.picturewindowbooks.com

Printed in the United States of America.

**Library of Congress Cataloging-in-Publication Data**
Jones, Christianne C.
How many spots does a leopard have? / by Christianne C. Jones ; illustrated by
Svetlana A. Zhurkina.
p. cm. — (Read-it! readers: folk tales)
Summary: Leopard offers a special prize to the one who can count all of his beautiful spots,
and is disappointed to find that many animals cannot count.
ISBN 1-4048-0973-2 (hardcover)
1. Tales—Africa. [1. Folklore—Africa.] I. Zhurkina, Svetlana, ill. II. Title. III. Series:
Read-it! readers folk tales.
PZ8.1.J646Ho 2004
398.24'5297554—dc22                                                    2004018441

To my daughter, Katia Tamara—S.A.Z.

# How Many Spots Does a Leopard Have?

By Christianne C. Jones

Illustrated by Svetlana A. Zhurkina

Special thanks to our advisers for their expertise:

Adria F. Klein, Ph.D.
Professor Emeritus, California State University
San Bernardino, California

Susan Kesselring, M.A.
Literacy Educator
Rosemount-Apple Valley-Eagan (Minnesota) School District

PiCTURE WiNDOW BOOKS
Minneapolis, Minnesota

One hot, sunny morning, Leopard
was admiring his reflection in the lake.

"How beautiful I am! My spots are amazing!" purred Leopard.

Suddenly, his reflection disappeared,
and Crocodile appeared in the lake.

"All you do is stare at yourself, Leopard. You probably spend all of your time counting your spots," growled Crocodile.

"What an excellent idea!" cried Leopard. "I wonder how many spots I have."

Since Leopard didn't know how to count, he asked Crocodile to help him.

"I have better things to do than count your spots!" Crocodile exclaimed and swam away.

"Crocodile doesn't know how to count, either," laughed Leopard.

Leopard went looking for someone to help him count. He ran into Weasel.

"Hello, Weasel. Will you please help me count my spots?" Leopard asked nicely.

13

"I can't count past four," Weasel said. "I'm sure one of the other animals can help you, if you ask nicely."

"Grand idea, Weasel! I will even give a prize to the animal who counts all of my spots!" Leopard declared.

Leopard and Weasel hurried down to the lake. "Attention!" yelled Leopard. "Any animal who can count all of my spots will win a special prize."

The animals became excited.

"I shall go first since I'm the oldest," announced Elephant. He got to ten and started over.

...1 2 3 4 5 6 7 8 9 10...

"You've already counted to ten!"
shouted the animals.

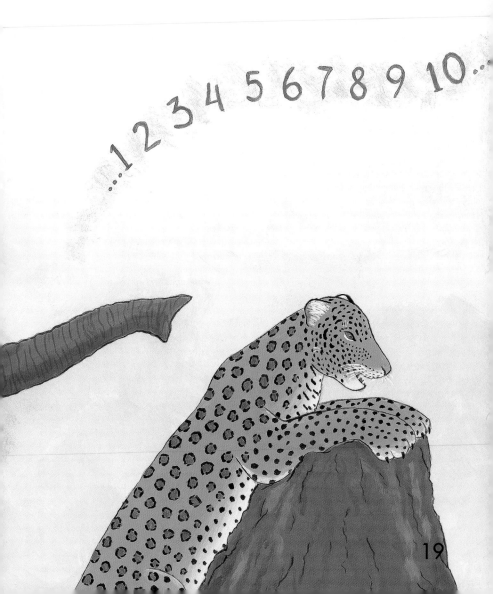

Elephant started over again and counted to ten twice. "Leopard has more than twenty spots," he said.

"How many more?" Leopard asked.

"A lot. In fact, I don't have time to count all of your spots," Elephant barked and marched away.

"Elephant can't count past twenty!"
shouted Mule.

"Can you count past twenty?" asked Leopard.

"Oh, no. I can only count to four because that's how many legs I have," explained Mule.

Bear decided to try, but he couldn't get past twenty-nine. "There are too many spots!" roared Bear.

"Can anyone help me?"
pleaded Leopard.

"Help with what?" squeaked Rabbit.

The animals told Rabbit what was going on.

"That is so easy!" bragged Rabbit.

Rabbit started to count Leopard's spots. "This one is dark. This one is light. Dark, light, dark, light," repeated Rabbit.

He kept going until he had counted all of Leopard's spots. "Leopard has only two spots," Rabbit concluded. "Light and dark."

29

The animals were impressed.

Leopard knew that wasn't quite right.

But he didn't know why, since he

couldn't count.

So, Rabbit received his special
prize—a picture of Leopard!

# More *Read-it!* Readers

Bright pictures and fun stories help you practice your reading skills. Look for more books at your level.

### FOLK TALES

*Chicken Little* by Christianne C. Jones

*The Gingerbread Man* by Eric Blair

*How Many Spots Does a Leopard Have?*
    by Christianne C. Jones

*The Little Red Hen* by Christianne C. Jones

*How the Camel Got Its Hump* by Christianne C. Jones

*The Pied Piper* by Eric Blair

*Stone Soup* by Christianne C. Jones

Looking for a specific title or level? A complete list of *Read-it!* Readers is available on our Web site: *www.picturewindowbooks.com*